THE ADVENTURES OF TOM SAWYER

Mark Twain

AWARD PUBLICATIONS LIMITED
LONDON

Aunt Polly

"Tom, Tom! Where are you?" There was no boy along the Mississippi who could disappear so completely as young Tom Sawyer. It was a mystery to his Aunt Polly how he did it.

The old lady pulled her spectacles down over her nose and looked over them, all round the room. She searched the house to make sure that Tom was not hiding under the bed or in the cupboard; then she went outside and stood in the doorway. She shouted, "Tom, Tom! Y-oou-u Tom!"

There was a sudden slight noise behind her and she whirled round just in time to seize a small boy by his jacket.

"Where've you been? What have you been doing?" she demanded. "Look at your hands and mouth – all covered with jam!"

"Nothing, Aunt," mumbled Tom.

Then, as she snatched up a switch to hit him with, he cried, "Hey! Look behind you!"

The old lady grasped her skirts, dropping her switch as she did so, and Tom fled, disappearing quickly over the high fence.

Aunt Polly lowered her skirts. "Hang the boy!" she said aloud. "He's forever getting the better of me. But he's my own poor dead sister's son and I must do my best for him."

Truth to tell, the old lady loved Tom as if he was her own son and it worried her that he was the naughtiest, wildest boy in the village – with scarcely an atom of learning in his head. Not that Tom was stupid; he just couldn't see the point of wasting beautiful summer days in the classroom.

Aunt Polly went back to her knitting – she knew Tom would not return that afternoon. But that night she waited up for him and, as he climbed quietly in at the window, she caught hold of him firmly. When she saw the state of his clothes, torn and dirty after a fight with another boy, she gave him a good shake.

"Tomorrow is Saturday," she said. "But it'll be no holiday for you. It's hard labour you'll be doing – whitewashing my fence. And not until it is all finished will you be free to play."

Tom groaned as he got up the next morning. Saturday! The day when he could go down to the river to watch the steamboats or hang round the village pump, talking and laughing with his friends. Instead he had to whitewash the fence!

After breakfast, Aunt Polly gave him a bucket of whitewash and a long-handled brush. "Now, get on with it," she said firmly.

Tom sighed deeply as he looked up at the fence. Then slowly he dipped his brush into the bucket of whitewash and slowly he passed it along the topmost plank.

some broken bits of toys, two marbles and a bent pin. There was simply nothing that would buy him more than ten minutes' freedom.

Then an idea came to him, an idea so brilliant that he whooped aloud. Once again he took up his brush, but this time his face bore the look of an artist who was doing exactly what he wanted to do. Out of the corner of his eye he saw one of his hated rivals approach. It was Ben Rogers – one of the few boys who could make Tom mad by poking fun at him. Now, as he drew near, he held out the round red apple he was eating and called, ''Hello, Tom, old friend! You got to work? Too bad and on Saturday, too!''

Tom went on whitewashing, paying no attention to anything but what he was doing. And at every gentle stroke of his brush, he smiled approvingly. He looked as if he was really enjoying himself.

Ben tried again. ''I'm going swimming. Don't you wish you could? But, of course, you'd rather work . . .''

''It all depends what you call work,'' Tom muttered.

''Why, what you're doing now, of course. That's work,'' returned Ben, looking slightly puzzled.

''All I know is, it suits Tom Sawyer,'' said Tom, gravely. ''Why, it's not every day a boy gets a chance to whitewash a fence like this.''

That put everything in a new light and Ben stopped nibbling his apple. Presently, he said, ''Say, Tom, let me whitewash a little.''

''No,'' said Tom, firmly, ''I'm afraid I can't do that. You see Aunt Polly's very particular about this fence. It's got to be done very carefully. I reckon there's scarcely a boy in a thousand, maybe even two thousand, who can do it in the way it's got to be done.''

''Is that so? Oh, come now, let me just try.'' Ben was in earnest now.

''Honest injun, Ben, I daren't . . .''

He had hardly made any progress when a small coloured boy came skipping out of the gate carrying a tin pail.

''Hallo, Jim,'' Tom greeted the boy.

''Can't stop, Mastah Tom,'' was Jim's reply. ''Missus tole me I got to go an git some water from the pump.''

''Gimme the pail,'' said Tom, who suddenly saw a way of getting down to the village. ''I'll fetch the water for you.''

''Missus Polly will whack me,'' said Jim, rolling his eyes, ''She'd take de head off me, she would!''

''Course she wouldn't,'' replied Tom. ''Look, I'll give you my best marble.''

Jim began to waver. He put down his pail and held out his hand for the treasure. The next minute, he was flying down the street with his pail and a tingling rear. And Tom was whitewashing the fence as if his life depended on it.

No sooner had his aunt disappeared into the house again than Tom put down his brush. Searching in his pockets, he brought out his entire worldly wealth –

"I'll give you my apple," said Ben. "What's left of it, anyway."

Tom pretended to hesitate. Then, with a doubtful look on his face, but with great glee in his heart, he gave Ben the brush. And while Ben worked, Tom sat down on a barrel in the shade, munching the apple and planning the next step in his campaign. By the time Ben was tired out, Tom had traded the next glorious chance to whitewash the fence to Billy Fisher for a kite, and, when he was exhausted, Johnny Miller bought his chance for a dead rat and a long piece of string.

By the middle of the afternoon, Tom had more treasures than he had ever had in his life. They included a tin soldier, a couple of tadpoles, a kitten with only one eye, a brass door-knob and a knife handle. Besides all this glorious wealth, he had had a lovely lazy time with plenty of company, and the fence had been given no less than three coats of whitewash.

Aunt Polly was dozing when Tom went in.

"May I go and play now, Aunt?" he asked. "The fence is all done."

"Tom, don't lie to me, I can't bear it," she said wearily.

"I'm not lying. I tell you, it's all done," said Tom.

The old lady, placing small trust in Tom's words, went outside to see for herself. When she found the whole fence whitewashed, not only once but three times, her astonishment was so great that she almost lost her voice.

At last she exclaimed, "Well, I never! You can work when you've a mind to, Tom.

Yes, go along and play. But mind you get back before it's dark.''

And she was so pleased with Tom that she took him into the kitchen, gave him one of her juiciest apples, and told him how good it was to do work honestly and well. And Tom, as he nodded and listened intently, managed to sneak a doughnut from the plate on the shelf and hide it away in his pocket before finally escaping out-of-doors.

Tom meets Huckleberry Finn

Monday morning found Tom Sawyer miserable. Mondays always found him so because it began another week's long suffering in school.

He lay and thought. He wished he was sick. He discovered that one of his teeth was loose, but his aunt would pull it out, and that would hurt.

No, he would keep the tooth in reserve and concentrate on something else. Perhaps a sore toe would do. He began to groan with considerable spirit, at the same time clutching his toe.

But Sid, his half-brother, slept on.

Tom was annoyed. He called, "Sid, Sid!" and then he shook him. Sid's snores stopped. Propping himself up on his elbow he stared at Tom. Tom went on groaning.

"Here, Tom! Tom! What's the matter?" Sid asked, stretching out a hand to him.

Tom moaned, "Oh, don't, Sid. Don't touch me!"

Sid was so worried he called out, "Oh, Aunt Polly, come quickly! Tom's dying!"

"Rubbish. I don't believe it!" she said. But she flew upstairs with Tom's cousin Mary.

When she reached the bedside she gasped out, "Now, Tom! Tom, what's the matter with you?"

"Oh, Auntie, I'm – it's my sore toe, it's mortified!"

The old lady sank down into a chair and laughed a little, then cried a little. "Tom, what a turn you did give me. Now you stop that nonsense and climb out of your bed."

The groans ceased and Tom began to feel a little foolish.

"Aunt Polly, it *seemed* mortified, and it hurt so I never minded my tooth . . ."

"Your tooth, indeed! What's the matter with your tooth?"

"It's loose, and it aches perfectly awful."

"Well, your tooth *is* loose," declared Aunt Polly, after a quick look. "Mary, get me a silk thread and a chunk of fire out of the kitchen."

Tom cried, "Oh, please, Auntie, don't pull it out. It doesn't hurt any more and I don't want to stay home from school."

But Aunt Polly was determined to pull out Tom's tooth. She tied one end of the silk thread to the tooth with a loop and tied the other end to the bedpost. Then she seized the chunk of fire and suddenly thrust it almost into Tom's face. In a twinkle the tooth hung dangling from the bedpost.

Later, as Tom walked to school, he was the envy of every boy he met because the gap in his teeth enabled him to spit in a new and admirable way.

Before he reached school, Tom met Huckleberry Finn. Huckleberry was idle, and lawless, and vulgar, and bad – and all the other children admired him and wished they dared be like him. Tom was under strict orders not to play with him. So he played with him every time he got a chance.

Huckleberry was always dressed in the cast-off clothes of full-grown men. His hat was floppy and tattered. Only one brace supported his trousers, which had a very baggy seat. The trouser legs were fringed and dragged in the dirt when not rolled up.

He slept on door-steps when it was fine, and in empty outhouses and sheds when it rained. He came and went as he pleased and did not have to go to school. He never had to wash or wear clean clothes and

altogether, in Tom's eyes, he led a perfect life. Tom was pleased to see him.

''Hallo, Huckleberry!''

''Hallo yourself and see how you like it,'' retorted Huckleberry.

''What's that you got?''

''Dead cat.''

''Lemme see him, Huck. My, he's pretty stiff. Where'd you get him?''

''Bought him off a boy.''

''What did you give?''

''A blue ticket and a bladder that I got at the slaughter-house.''

''Where'd you get the blue ticket?''

''Bought it off'n Ben Rogers two weeks ago for a hoopstick.''

Tom digested this piece of information. Then he asked, ''What is dead cats good for, Huck?''

''Good for? Cure warts with,'' said Huck, knowingly.

''How d'you cure warts with cats?'' inquired Tom, with disbelief in his voice.

''Why, you take your cat and go to the graveyard, round about midnight, where somebody that was wicked has been buried. And when it's midnight a devil will come, maybe two or three, but you can't see 'em, you can only hear something like the wind, or maybe hear 'em talk; and when they're taking that feller away, you heave your cat after 'em and say, 'Devil follow corpse, cat follow devil, warts follow cat. I'm done with ye!' That'll cure *any* wart.''

Tom thought for a minute. Then he said, ''Sounds all right, Huck. When you going to try the cat?''

''Tonight. I reckon they'll come after old Hoss Williams tonight,'' Huck answered.

''Lemme go with you!' Tom said eagerly.

''Of course – if you ain't afeard,'' was the somewhat sneering reply.

''Afeard! Tain't likely! Will you meow?''

''Yes, and you meow back if you get a chance,'' Huck told him.

And Tom continued on his way to school.

When he reached the schoolhouse the master saw him at once.

"Thomas Sawyer!" he boomed sternly.

"Sir!"

"Come up here. Now, sir. As usual you are late. What is the reason this time?"

Tom was about to tell a lie when he saw two long tails of yellow hair; they belonged to a new girl and there was a vacant place beside her.

He said instantly, "I stopped to talk with Huckleberry Finn!"

The master stared helplessly.

"Thomas Sawyer, this is the most astounding confession I've ever listened to," said the master. "Remove your jacket."

The master whacked Tom soundly. Then he gave the order, "Now, sir, go and sit with the *girls!*"

A titter rippled round the room, but Tom didn't mind. He sat down beside the girl with the yellow hair.

Presently Tom began to steal furtive glances at the girl. Then he drew something on his slate, hiding his work with his left hand. For a time she took no notice. Then, after a little while, curiosity overcame her and she whispered hesitatingly, "Let me see."

Tom partly uncovered a rather poor drawing of a house with two gable ends and a cork-screw of smoke issuing from the chimney.

She gazed at it for a moment then whispered, "It's ever so nice. I wish I could draw."

"It's easy," whispered Tom. "I'll learn you. What's your name?"

"Becky Thatcher."

"And I'm Tom Sawyer." As he spoke, Tom began to scrawl something on the slate, hiding the words from Becky.

At her entreaties, Tom began letting his hand slip by degrees away from the slate till what he had written was clearly revealed. It said, "I love you."

"Oh, you bad thing!" Becky exclaimed. And she hit his hand a smart rap, but reddened and looked pleased anyway.

When school broke up at noon, Tom whispered to Becky to meet him before going home.

In a little while the two met at the bottom of the lane. They walked together back towards the schoolhouse. Then they sat, side by side, with a slate before them.

Tom drew a picture of a house, not unlike the one he had drawn earlier in class. It wasn't good, but Becky liked it.

Tom gave Becky the pencil. He held his hand over hers, guiding it, and so created another drawing of a house.

Then Tom drew a picture of a man standing beside the house. This was more difficult but Becky was keen to learn how to do this too.

Presently Tom asked, ''Becky, was you ever engaged?''

''What's that?''

''Why, engaged to be married.''

''No.''

''Would you like to?''

Becky nodded and Tom passed his arm

about her waist and whispered some sweet words into her ears.

"It's ever so much fun being engaged," he said. "Why, me and Amy Lawrence, we . . ."

Becky's eyes widened and Tom realised his blunder, but it was too late. Becky began to cry and, as her sobs grew louder, he got out his most prized jewel, a brass knob from the top of a fire-guard.

"Please, Becky, take this."

She threw it to the floor. At that, Tom stood up and marched out of the school-house, over the hills and far away, to return to school no more that day.

"Tom! Come back, Tom!" Becky entreated through her tears. And when he did not, she sat down and cried again.

Tom's midnight adventure

Tom spent the rest of the day in the woods, and by the time he got back home he had forgotten Becky.

At half-past nine that night he and Sid were sent to bed as usual. They said their prayers and Sid was soon asleep. Tom lay

awake for a while, tossing in restless impatience, but, in spite of himself, he began to doze. When the clock chimed eleven, he did not hear it.

Suddenly, mingling with his half-formed dreams, he heard a most melancholy caterwauling. He was soon wide awake, dressed and out of the window. Huckleberry Finn was waiting for him with his dead cat. Half-an-hour later they were wading through the tall grass of the graveyard.

A faint wind moaned through the trees and Tom was thankful when they found the new heap of earth they were looking for.

They hid behind the three great elms that grew next to this grave.

They waited in silence until, suddenly, Tom seized Huck's arm and said, ''Ssh!''

Huckleberry whispered nervously, ''What is it, Tom?''

''Ssh! There 'tis again. Didn't you hear it?'' Tom said.

''Lord, Tom, they're coming! They're coming, sure as anything. What'll we do? They can see in the dark, same as cats . . .''

The boys scarcely breathed. A muffled sound of voices floated up from the far end of the graveyard.

"Look! See there!" whispered Tom. "What is it?"

"It's devil-fire. Oh, Tom, this is awful," groaned Huckleberry.

Some figures approached through the gloom, swinging an old-fashioned tin lantern. Huckleberry whispered with a shudder, "It's the devils, sure enough. Three of 'em. Lordy, Tom, we're goners!"

"I'll try to pray. Don't you be afeard," Tom whispered back.

Then Huck exclaimed softly, "They're *humans*! One of 'em is, anyway. One of 'em is old Muff Potter's voice."

Tom listened intently. "Say, Huck, I know another o' them voices – it's Injun Joe," he said.

"That's so – that murderin' rascal! I'd rather they was devils," muttered Huck.

"What ever can they be up to?"

By now the three men had reached the grave.

"Here it is," said the third voice; and the boys saw young Dr. Robinson.

Potter and Injun Joe began to shovel earth out of the grave.

"Hurry, men!" said the doctor in a low voice. "The moon might come out."

They growled a response and went on digging. Finally, one of them struck upon the coffin with a dull, woody noise. The men hoisted it out on to the ground. They prised off the lid with their shovels, got out the body and dumped it on the ground. Just at that moment, the moon drifted out from behind the clouds and the boys saw the face. The corpse was placed on a barrow, covered with a blanket and bound

with a rope. Then Potter took out a spring-knife and cut off the end of the rope.

"Now the cussed thing's ready, Saw-bones," he said. "And you'll just out with another five, or here it stays."

"That's the talk!" said Injun Joe.

"Look here; what does this mean?" said the doctor. "You required your pay in advance and I've paid you."

"Yes, and you done more than that," said Injun Joe, approaching the doctor. "Five years ago your father had me jailed for a tramp when I come begging for food. Did you think I'd forget? And now I've got you and you got to settle!"

He was threatening the doctor with his fist in his face by this time. The doctor struck out suddenly and stretched the ruffian on the ground.

"Here, no, don't you strike Joe!" Potter exclaimed, dropping the knife. The next moment he was grappling with the doctor and the two were struggling with might and main.

Injun Joe sprang to his feet, his eyes flaming with passion as he snatched up Potter's knife.

Suddenly, the doctor flung himself free, seized the heavy headboard of the grave and felled Potter to the ground with it. In the same instant Injun Joe drove the knife to its hilt in the young man's breast. The doctor reeled and fell across Potter, covering him with his blood. The two frightened boys crept away in the dark as fast as they dared.

Injun Joe quickly robbed the doctor's body of all its belongings and after that he

put the fatal knife in Potter's open right hand. Then he sat down on the dismantled coffin. Three – four – maybe five minutes passed before Potter began to stir and moan. His hand closed upon the knife and he held it up and looked at it. Instantly, he let it fall with a shudder and sat up, pushing the body from him. He gazed at it and then around him, looking confused.

"It's a dirty business," said Joe, without moving. "What did you do it for?"

"Me! I never done it," replied Potter.

"That kind of talk won't wash," Joe said.

Potter trembled. "I didn't know what I was a-doing," he muttered. "It must have been all that whisky I drunk. You won't tell, will you, Joe? You won't tell?"

"No, I won't go back on you, Muff Potter," said Joe.

"Oh, Joe, bless you!" Potter cried.

"Come, man," said Injun Joe. "No blubbering. You be off yonder way and I'll go this. Don't leave any tracks behind you."

Meanwhile, Tom and Huck were running on and on towards the village, terrified that they might be followed. They didn't dare to look behind them.

"If we can only get to the old tannery before we break down!" whispered Tom, in short catches between breaths.

At last they burst through the tannery's open door and lay down exhausted.

After what seemed like an hour, but was in fact only ten minutes, their hearts had stopped banging and they were able to speak normally.

Finally Tom whispered, "What do you reckon'll come of it?"

"I reckon hanging'll come of it," retorted Huck.

Tom thought awhile, then he said, "Who'll tell? Us?"

"What are you talking about?" Huck burst out. "If something happened and Injun Joe didn't hang, why he'd kill us

Huck Finn and Tom Sawyer swears they will keep mum about this and they wish they may Drop down dead in their tracks if they ever tell and Rot.
T.S.   H.F.

some time or other, just as dead sure as we're a-lying here. Tom, we got to keep mum," he said gravely. "That Injun devil wouldn't make any more of drowning us than a couple of cats. There orter be writing 'bout this. And blood."

Tom agreed wholeheartedly. He found a clean block of pine wood and a little fragment of ochre dye from his pocket.

Then he painfully scrawled their oath.

Each boy pricked the ball of his thumb and squeezed out a drop of blood. Tom showed the admiring Huckleberry how to make an H and an F, after he had signed his own initials, and the oath was complete. They buried the block close to the wall and knew they would not speak of it to anyone.

Tom
runs away

The whole village was horrified by the ghastly news of the young doctor's murder. A gory knife had been found close to the murdered man and it had been identified as belonging to Muff Potter.

Tom and Huckleberry joined the crowd that had gathered in the graveyard. The

boys shivered when they saw Injun Joe.
The sheriff arrived, leading Potter by the
arm. The poor fellow's eyes showed his
fear.

"I didn't do it, friends," he sobbed.
And when he saw Injun Joe he shouted,
"Tell 'em, Joe, tell 'em!"

Huckleberry and Tom stood dumb-
founded and staring as they heard the
stony-hearted liar reel off his statement
about the fight, with never a word about
his own terrible part in it.

Later, at the inquest, Injun Joe repeated
his lies and Muff Potter was thrust into jail
to await trial.

Tom felt very bad about this and every
day or two he went to the little jail window
and smuggled food through to the
"murderer". There were no guards, so
Tom could come and go without being
seen by anyone.

One day, when Aunt Polly had been

scolding him more than usual, Tom
decided to run away.

He set off and had not gone far when he
met his friend, Joe Harper. Joe, too, was
miserable and dejected, having been
punished unjustly by his mother for something he hadn't done.

As the two boys walked along the bank
of the Mississippi River, they began to
make plans.

The boys agreed that they would
become pirates and live a life of crime.
Jackson's Island was not far off – it was
wooded and uninhabited. It would make
ideal headquarters for pirates.

This settled, they hunted up Huckleberry Finn and told him of their plans. He
promptly joined them.

Then the three separated. They had
agreed that proper pirates did everything
under the cover of darkness; they would
meet again at a lonely spot on the river

bank at the magic hour of midnight.

It was starlight, and very still, when Tom arrived with a boiled ham and some bread at the meeting place. He squatted down behind a tree at the top of the riverbank. He listened a moment before giving a low, distinct whistle. It was answered from the darkness below. Then a guarded voice said, ''Who goes there?''

''Tom Sawyer, the Black Avenger of the Spanish Main. Name your names,'' said Tom, gravely.

''Huck Finn the Red-handed and Joe Harper the Terror of the Seas,'' came the reply.

''''Tis well. Give the countersign.''

Two hoarse whispers delivered the same awful word together: ''BLOOD!''

Then Tom scrambled down to his waiting comrades. The Terror of the Seas had brought a side of bacon, and Finn the Red-handed produced a skillet, some half-cured leaf tobacco and a few corn-cobs to make pipes with. However, none of the pirates but himself smoked or "chewed". The Black Avenger of the Spanish Main said it would never do to start without a boat, and they saw a raft a little distance away. They crept stealthily down to the raft and shoved off; Tom in command, Huck at the after oar and Joe at the for'ard. Tom stood amidships, gloomy-browed and with folded arms, and gave his orders in a low, stern whisper.

About two o'clock in the morning the raft reached the island and the intrepid pirates landed their freight. The old sail was spread out like a tent to shelter the provisions. The pirates themselves would sleep in the open air.

They built a fire inside the dark forest and then cooked some bacon in the frying-pan for supper. It seemed glorious sport to be feasting in that wild free way in the forest and on an island far from the haunts of men.

"This is the life for me," said Tom. "You don't have to get up mornings and you don't have to go to school, and wash, and all that foolishness."

Huck began to blow out a cloud of fragrant smoke from his cob pipe. Then he asked, "What does pirates have to do?"

"Oh, they just have a bully-time," Tom said. "They take ships and burn them, and get the money and bury it in awful places in their island where there's ghosts and things to watch it, and kill everybody in the ships – make 'em walk a plank."

As they talked, the pipe dropped from the fingers of the Red-handed and he slept. But the Terror of the Seas and the Black Avenger of the Spanish Main had more trouble in getting to sleep. They were not so used to sleeping rough!

Early the next morning Tom stirred up the other pirates. In a minute or two they were all stripped and they chased after and tumbled over each other in the shallow water near their camp.

They cooked breakfast on the camp fire

and then there was the whole day left to explore the island.

Late in the afternoon, a muffled boom startled all three of them and they sprang to their feet and ran to the shore. They parted the bushes on the bank and peered out over the water. They saw the little steam ferry-boat some way below the village, drifting with the current. Her broad deck seemed crowded with people, and there were a great many skiffs rowing about or floating with the stream near the ferry-boat. Presently, a great jet of white smoke burst from the ferry-boat's side.

''I know what it's all about,'' Tom suddenly shouted. ''Somebody's drownded!''

''That's it,'' said Huck. ''They shoot a cannon over the water and that makes the drownded man come up to the top . . .''

The boys watched intently. Then Tom suddenly cried, ''Boys, I know who's drownded: it's us!''

The pirates returned to camp, full of pride at the trouble they were making. But when the shadows of night closed them in, their excitement vanished, and Tom and Joe could not keep back thoughts of their families who were not enjoying this fine frolic as much as they were. Presently Huck and Joe fell asleep, but Tom did not. At last he rose cautiously: he had something to do.

It was broad daylight before Tom reappeared at the camp site. Over a sumptuous breakfast of bacon and fish he recounted his adventures and told them his plan. He had sneaked back home and seen the grief of Aunt Polly and Joe's mother who believed they were all ''drownded''. He had heard them say that the funerals would be in two days' time, on Sunday.

Tom's great plan was to return home with his brother pirates and attend their own funerals.

Accordingly, at dusk on the Saturday, they paddled over to the Missouri shore on a log and slept in the woods on the edge of the town till nearly daylight. Then they

made their way to the unused gallery of the church to await events.

As the bell began to toll, the villagers crowded into the little church. Then Aunt Polly entered, followed by Sid and Mary, and then by the Harper family, all in deep black. The whole congregation and the old minister rose reverently and stood until the mourners were seated in the front pew.

As the service proceeded, the boys crept down from the gallery; a moment later the church door creaked. The minister raised his eyes. As he stared at the door he stopped talking, but his mouth remained wide open. And then, all at once, the con-gregation turned and stared while the three dead boys came up the aisle – Tom in the lead, Joe next, and Huck sneaking sheepishly in the rear.

Aunt Polly, Mary and the Harpers threw themselves upon Tom and Joe, smothering them with kisses, while poor Huck stood abashed and uncomfortable. As he started to slink away, Tom seized him.

"Aunt Polly, it ain't fair," he cried. "Somebody's got to be glad to see Huck."

"And so they shall!" cried Aunt Polly. But the loving attentions the old lady now lavished upon the outcast made him even more uncomfortable than he had been!

Buried treasure

For the remainder of the school term, Tom was the hero of the hour. Only one thing marred his otherwise carefree days. This was Muff Potter's trial for murder. Tom hung about the court-room, unable to tear himself away and, when at last he was convinced that poor Muff Potter would be found guilty, he asked to be called as witness for the defence.

The sight of Injun Joe's iron face made Tom shiver but, somehow or other, he got started on his story.

All eyes were on him as he said, "And as the doctor swung the board around and Muff Potter fell, Injun Joe jumped with the knife and . . ."

Crash! Quick as lightning, the halfbreed sprang from his seat, tore his way through all opposers and was gone!

Tom was a glittering hero once more, but his dreams were haunted by Injun Joe coming to take his revenge, and he wished with all his heart that he could be captured.

The holidays came. Tom's true love, Becky, went away and Tom turned his mind to other matters. Hidden treasure was one.

"We'll dig for it on Cardiff Hill," he said to Huck one morning, "under the old dead tree that stands there on the top."

Huck was delighted and, armed with a rusty old pick and a shovel, the two set out to tramp to the site.

They dug a number of holes without finding as much as an old bone. They decided to go down the hill to the haunted house to see what they could find there.

It was a crumbling, derelict place and when they reached it they were afraid for a moment to venture in.

But there were two of them and each felt he must be braver than the other, so they entered and went upstairs. Finding nothing of interest though, they were about to go down again when Tom

suddenly said, "Ssh!"

"What is it?" whispered Huck, fearfully.

"Ssh! There! Hear it? Keep still. They're coming right towards the door downstairs," Tom said softly.

The boys stretched themselves upon the floor with their eyes to knot-holes in the planking, and they lay waiting in a cloud of fear.

Two men entered. One of them, an old Spaniard, was wrapped in a blanket. He had bushy white whiskers and long white hair, and he wore green goggles. The boys recognised the other man when he spoke. It was the voice of Injun Joe!

The two men began talking about burying their swag, "six hundred and fifty in silver", and the boys forgot all their fears as they saw Joe, on his knees, in the corner digging with his bowie-knife. They nudged each other in their gloating excitement.

Suddenly Joe's knife struck something.

"Hallo," he said. "Here's a half-rotten plank – no, it's a box. I've broke a hole."

He reached his hand in and drew it out.

"Man, it's money!" he exclaimed.

The two villains examined the gold coins and the Spaniard said, "We'll make swift work of this. I just saw an old pick."

He ran and brought over Tom's pick and shovel. Very soon the box was opened. "There's thousands of dollars here. We'll take it to our den – number two, under the cross," said Injun Joe.

As they slipped out of the house in the deepening twilight, Tom and Huck rose up, weak but vastly relieved. They had not been seen. Now all they had to do was to track down the iron-bound box and the treasure would be theirs!

In the days that followed, Tom made a hundred and one plans as to how to track down the iron-bound box. But then something happened that made Injun Joe and the treasure become less important.

Becky was home again. Judge Thatcher had chartered an old ferry-boat and a

picnic would be held for her friends down-river on Friday.

Tom was in a fever of excitement, when Friday morning dawned, clear and bright.

"I tell you what," he said to Becky, as they tripped along. "We'll climb Cardiff Hill and then we'll stop at Widow Douglas's place. She'll have ice-cream, and she'll be awfully glad to have us. She'll be glad to put us both up at the end of the picnic and that'll save you spending the night at the Harper's like your Ma said."

Becky agreed somewhat doubtfully, as they boarded the ferry. Sometime later the crowd of laughing boys and girls swarmed ashore, and after some games, a feast was spread out and devoured in the shade of spreading oaks.

Presently somebody shouted, "Who's ready for the cave?"

Everybody was and, as bundles of candles were produced, there was a general scamper up the hill.

McDougal's Cave was a maze of crooked aisles that ran into each other and out again and led nowhere. Tom knew as much of the cave as anyone.

With Becky at his side, Tom followed the rest. They did not immediately notice that they had wandered off and were alone. On and on they went, far down into the cave's secret depths until, finally, they found themselves in a cavern.

Under the roof thousands of bats had packed themselves and, as the light from the candles disturbed them, they came flocking down, squeaking furiously. They darted at the candles and Becky's went out. She shivered.

"We'd better start back, Tom," she whispered. "I hope we won't get lost."

But the bats had chased them a good distance and before long Tom knew, with sinking heart, they were hopelessly lost.

The began wandering aimlessly until they came upon a spring. Worn out and hungry, Becky sank to the ground.

"They're sure to miss us soon," Tom

comforted her. Then he remembered that her mother thought she was spending the night at the Harper's house, and his courage all but ebbed away.

The weary time dragged on; they slept a little and awoke famished and frightened. Perhaps it would be better to explore some of the side passages, rather than sit helplessly waiting, Tom thought. He took a length of string from his pocket, tied it to a rock and he and Becky started, Tom in the lead, unwinding the string as he groped along. At the end of twenty steps the corridor ended in a ''jumping-off'' place. Tom got down on his knees and felt below, and then as far around the corner as he could.

Then he saw, hardly any distance away, a human hand, holding a candle, appear from behind a rock! Tom's joyous shout

faded on his lips as he saw the body that followed the hand: it belonged to Injun Joe! For a moment he was paralysed. Then to his intense relief he realised that the half-breed had not seen him and, returning quickly to Becky, he led her back to the spring without telling her what he had seen.

The next passage Tom tried rewarded him beyond his wildest hope. There, far-off, was a speck that looked like daylight. He groped forward, pushed his head and shoulders through a small hole, and saw the broad Mississippi rolling by.

The two children crawled out wearily into the sunlight. Some men came along in a skiff, saw them and took them aboard. By nightfall, they were safely back home and the whole village went wild with joy.

When Becky gave her account of the

story, Tom came out of it so well that he was a hero. Everyone said how brave and clever he was and Aunt Polly was delighted that he had come home safely and soundly at last.

Huckleberry, too, had had success on the day of the picnic; he had overheard Injun Joe and the Spaniard planning to rob Widow Douglas who lived alone outside the village.

Huck had gone straight to the sheriff, who had raised the alarm amongst the village men. A posse had set off after the villains and in the chase Joe had escaped while the Spaniard had drowned in the river. Out of gratitude, the widow had taken Huck into her own house.

All this Tom learnt with some considerable amazement. But it was only later – two whole weeks later – that he learnt something else that drove the colour from his cheeks and left him white and trembling.

Two weeks later Tom was on his way to visit Huck when he stopped at Judge Thatcher's house to see Becky.

The judge said to him, "Well, Tom, nobody will get lost in that cave any more. I had its door sheathed with iron two weeks ago and triple locked; and I've got the keys."

And Tom, nearly fainting away, at last found the strength to mutter, "Oh, Judge, Injun Joe's in the cave!"

The treasure-seekers strike gold

The news spread in an amazingly short time and soon men, including Judge Thatcher and Tom, were hurrying up to McDougal's Cave. When the door was unlocked they saw a sorrowful sight. Injun Joe lay stretched upon the ground, dead, with his face close to the crack of the door and, by his side, was his knife, its blade broken in two. Tom's feelings were a mixture of pity and relief.

Tom took Huck aside.

"Huck," he said, "I know where the

money is. It's in the cave. It's a long way in, but there's a mighty short cut that nobody knows about but me. Will you come, Huck?''

''Let's start right off, Tom,'' Huck said.

Soon after noon, Tom proudly showed Huck the hole among the thick bushes where he and Becky had escaped from the cave.

Then they entered, Tom in the lead. They toiled their way to the farther end of the tunnel and to the spring. They pressed on until they reached the ''jumping-off'' place.

Tom held his candle aloft and said, ''Now, Huck, look as far around the corner as you can. Look on the big rock over yonder, marked with candle smoke.''

''Oh, it's a *cross*!'' exclaimed Huck.

''Exactly right,'' said Tom. ''It's *the* cross where Injun Joe buried the money box. I bet you the money is *under* the rock. I'm going to dig in the clay.''

His knife was out at once and he had hardly begun to dig when he struck wood. Soon he uncovered some boards, which Huck helped him to remove. They had concealed a natural chasm which led under the rock. Tom got into this and held his candle as far under the rock as he could and suddenly he exclaimed, ''My goodness, Huck, looky here!''

It was the treasure-box sure enough, occupying a snug little cavern along with an empty powder-keg, a couple of guns in leather, two or three pairs of old moccasins and a leather belt.

''Got it at last,'' said Huck, ploughing